Someone Special

Flairs and Glairs
Publication House

"Someone Special"

ISBN No: " 9789391302016"
1st Edition
Language – English and Hindi

Flairs and Glairs
Publication House
Regd. Under MSME Act.

Disclaimer

This is a work of fiction and solely represent the thoughts of the corresponding authors of the articles. Our editors have tried their best to edit the content of all the authors and check the plagiarism.

All the write-ups in this book are unique and are only published in this book.

In case any plagiarism or error is found, only the author is responsible alone, and not the publisher or the Compilers.

Cover Designing and Book Formatting
Shubham Shah and Ishani Agarwal

Acknowledgement

I would like to Thank my family for everything.
I don't think without your support, anything would have been possible.
My family did everything for me.
Apart from my family, My closest friends Siddhi, Trupti, Rutuja,Rushab Bhavesh, Abhishek& Mayuri plays an important role in my writing.
As per this book,I would Thank Ishani Di & Shivangi Di Shubham Shah, the founder of the publishing house, thank you for helping and supporting the way you did.Shubham Shah & Shivangi Jaiswal, without your support, I wouldn't have been standing here.
Thank You for all you have done. Kudos to your dedication.
Lastly, my Appreciation goes to my Co-Authors without your love,support and help this wouldn't be possible
Thank you for helping me in this beautiful journey by beingso patient, and completing our book in such a short span of time.

Co Author

Shubham Shah (Founder Flairs and Glairs)
Ishani Agarwal (Co-Founder Flairs and Glairs)
Nishiket R Surwade (Compiler)

1 - Priya Singh
2 - Ankita Deb
3 - Arshnoor
4 - Jyotsna Vyas
5 - Ankita Arsiya
6 - Payal Indani
7 - Pooja J. Indani
8 - Riya Srivastava
9 - Nr. Mrunal Hatwar
10 - Ritika Nagar
11 - Biswadeep Sen
12 - Prasenjit Raut
13 - आशीष "कृष्णा
14 - Santosh Chawan
15 - Raminder Kaur Mac
16 - Payal Singhal
17 - Saloni Kumari
18 - Ishrat Saboon
19 - Ganesh Sadashiv Patil
20 - Shivani Shrikant Sarwade
21 - Prakhar Mishra
22 - Prachi Sharma
23 - Akshat Kumar
24 - Mausam Agrawal
25 - Aditi Malviya
26 - Muskan Sahu
27 - Isha

28 - Sweety Akankshya Panda
29 - Akriti Sharma
30 - Shivani Priyanga
31 - Priyanka Sharma
32 - Gurdeep Kaur
33 - Komal Singh
34 - Reshma Sultana
35 - Tanvi Jamwal
36 - Utkarsh Devale
37 - Maniska Das
38 - Priyanka Yadav
39 - Agrima Viraj
40 - Avneet Kaur
41 - Pooja
42 - Himanshu Ranjan
43 - Ashis Pahi
44 - Priyanshi Mittal
45 - Navjot Singh
46 - T. Priyadharshini
47 - Vishal K R
48 - Aditi Kumari
49 - Himanshu Chaturvedi
50 - Husaina S

Shubham Shah

(Founder - Flairs and Glairs)

Shubham Shah, an entrepreneur at "Flairs & Glairs" a brand with dynamics in events organizing and cultural educational pan INDIA, is a 26yrs old guy who recently has entered the digital platform of imprinting emotions. He has initiated with his own open mic platform to help budding poets and aspiring writers under his brand named as "Teekhe Zasbaaat"

He is a commerce graduate from the Bhagalpur City of Bihar. He states Writing has impersonated him since childhood and he has now been writing for over a decade!
Cooking, on the other hand, is his passion! He also mentions, trying out new things just tickles him!
When asked sir, Why SPICY EMOTIONS?
He smiled and added, "agar jasbaat teekhe na ho toh wo jasbaat kahan" Spices are all that blends! So do his words!
As a chef, he presents to you his dish! Hot and freshly served! Taste it! Feel it! Enjoy it! You can also find his writing in the Book "Teekhe Zasbaaat" and 50+ Co -authored anthologies. With his passion to explore opportunities across Platforms, he is working with keen dev otion and We wish him all the very best for his future ventures.
He is Featured in the International Magazine DeMode for his upcoming solo novel.
He is Approved by Ne8x for its Lit Fest, and is a Golden Star Awards 2020 Winner.
He is a India Book of Records Holder for his Anthology Satrang, and has the Grandmaster title by Asia Book of Records, for the same.
He has also been featured in Prabhat Khabar, Dainik Jagran, and a lot of other Newspapers in Bihar for his achievements.
He has been a proud co-author to
India Book Of Records (Title- Black)
World Book Of Records (Title -15 Wonders of Poetries)
India Book Of Records (Title - Aaina)
Vajra World Records Holder (Title - Gustakhi Maaf Hai)
High Range of Records Holder (Title - Gustakhi Maaf Hai)
Indian Book of Records
(Title - Road from Worst to Best)

Share your reviews on his

INSTAGRAM

@spicy_emotions
@shubham4shah

Or via email on

shubham2shah@gmail.com

To stay tuned to his work and opportunities follow his business Handles

INSTAGRAM FACEBOOK YOUTUBE

@flairsandglairs
@teekhezasbaaat

WEBSITE:

https://flairsandglairs.in/
https://flairsandglairs.com/

Ishani Agarwal

(Co-Founder- Flairs and Glairs)

Ishani Agarwal hails from the City of Joy, Kolkata.
She is the co -founder of her Community "Teekhe Zasbaaat" and Flairs and Glairs Publication.
Been a Compiler for 45+ Anthologies, she is in the process for more. Co-authored in 150+ Anthologies. She is a India Book of Records Holder, a Vajra World Records Holder, a High Range of Records Holder, an OMG Book of Records Holder, a Bravo Record holder, a Forever Star Book of World Records and an Indian Book of Records Holder.
Approved by Ne8x for its Lit Fest 2020, and Literary Icon 2020. Also a Golden Star Awards Winner 2020.
She has also been award ed with India Star Republic Award 2021, a part of She Awards by Awards Arc and Winner of Nari Samman 2021 by Literoma.

She is also selected as Best Achiever of the Year by AwardsArc and Most Challenging Compiler Award by Spectrum Awards.
She got her first solo Published,a solo Compilation consisting of first 750 contents of hers, titled "Hand That Burnt While Healing".

She has been featured by the National Magazine "Taree Zameen Par" with the title 'unstoppable'.
Also featured in the International Magazine DeMode for her upcoming solo novel, she is proud to write on social issues, and is happy with the love she is receiving.
Connect with her on Instagram: @Ishani_agarwal_quotes / @compilations_so_far

Nishiket R Surwade
(Compiler)

Mr.Nishiket R Surwade,born on 24th july 1999 .He is a student pursuing his engineering in electronics and telecommunication field, Nashik, Maharashtra & Also a Project Co- Ordinator at "Flairs & Glairs"He is very shy and simple, easily make friends. He is a blogger and future E&TC engineer. He aspires to become IES Officer.

He has started writing as a career since he was in 12th std.He loves to write quote and shayri in Hindi as well as in English language. He loves to write about 'True love' He worked as co-author in some anthologies like 'The Broken Bond', 'For the name of love' and in more than 50 Anthologies. and also, being a compiler of the book "College Romance", "Life Sahi Hai" and many are in process

Meri Zindagi Ki Prerna Ho Tum

Meri Zindagi Ki Aarzoo Ho Tum,
Meri Khushiyon Ka Rasta Ho Tum.
Maana Ki Baatein Nahin Hoti Tumse Meri,
Lekin Dil Har Pal, Tumhe Hi Yaad Karta Hai Mera.

Main Kagaj Hoon,
To Meri Kalam Ho Tum.
Main Shayar,
To Meri Shayri Ho Tum.
Andhere Main Diya ,
To Uski Baati Ho Tum.
Meri Zindagi Main,
Aage Badhne Ki Prerna Ho Tum.

Pata Hai Naa Tum Ho Koi Pari Naa Koi Hoor,
Lekin Tum Hi Ho Meri Nazron Main Kohinoor.
Jisse Baat Karte Hi Mile Dil Ko Sukoon,
Wo Ho Tum.
Jiska Khayal Aate Hi Chehre Par Muskan Aa Jaye,
Wo Ho Tum.

Meri Khushiyon Ki Taale Ki Chabi Ho Tum,
Meri Aasha , Meri Ummid Ho Tum,
Haan Tum Meri Zindagi Ki Prerna Ho Tum....

Priya Singh

This is Priya Singh from Lucknow. she completed her graduation last year from Lucknow University and doing preparation for masters of business administration (MBA) apart from this she started writing quotes and shayri on quotes app after this i got this chance to write in book as a co -author ☺. She is also working as a meakup artist and digital creator.

Find Someone

Find Someone Who
Isn't Afraid To Admit
That They Miss You.
Someone Who
Knows That You Are
Not Perfect But
Treat You As If You
Are. Someone
Who's Biggest Fear
Is Loosing You.One
Who Gives Their
Heart Completely.
Someone Who Said
'I LOVE YOU' And
Means It.Someone
Who Knows Your
Mood Swings. Last
But Not Least,Find
Someone Who Wouldn't
Mind Waking Up
With You It The
Morning And Seeing You
In Wrinkles And Your Grey
Hair But Still Falls
For You All Over Again

Don't Let Her Go

She was a forgiver.
Her heart was so large.
She didn't Know
How to give up on
People, because she always
Believed that good is those
She loved. It was until
She was walked on so
Many times,she had no choice
But to let go of those who burned
Holes in her heart.
Don't let her go she was a forgiver

Ankita Deb

She is a teenager girl of 17 hailing from Assam, the land of natural beauty.A student of humanities who loves literature above everything.She has been writing since seven years and her love for nature is specially visible in most of her poems. She likes exploring new things such as painting, debat ing, delivering speeches, appearing in quiz competition, reciting poems and story telling. She is an optimistic soul and a dreamer.

Reminiscence Of Unloved Tale

I'll bloom today for you,
Feeling the essence of your flower like heart with vibrant hue.
I'll step out, being the evidence of the glorious bond of us that began from dawn,
I would love to see the height of the flying butterflies in my stomach that perched on your little frown.
Seeing you writing a note on the leaves for the apology of memories which are already gone!
My call from the heart that you received ,relived the love that has just begun.
Relentlessly travelling on each other's thoughts in mind,
But our love has logic too, as we threw colours on age old the notion of "love is blind!"
You sat under the tree constantly staring in my shinning eyes with extreme innocence,
You told me! You're finding the pen which has written a milestone of our existence.
My beats of heart weren't so special till then,
After your arrival, you composed a song out of our heartbeats catching in the air frame.
Your busy days vehemently shattered the tale into pieces,
Later my mind realised,it was the illusion of my stupid heart that you were loving me back those days!
When my reality evolved as an illusion,
My entire life imagining without you seemed like a ray of hallucination.
I can't even remain myself,
Reminiscence of my collapsed castle was snatched by the words of your loving self.
Can't even say I hate you
But yeah! Apart from letting my dry cracked heart die,I chose to unlove you!

Arshnoor

Arshnoor kaur
An introvert girl who expresses feelings by writing...

(1)

Apni Aankhon Mein, Kisi Aur Ko Basa Na Dena...
Mere Siwa Kisi Aur Ko, Apni Wafa Na Dena...

Tera Khwaab, Teri Chahat, Teri Aarzoo Hoon Main...
Mujhe Zindagi Mein Kabhi, Bhula Na Dena...

Hadd Se Jyaada, Bas Tumhi Ko Chaha Hai
Pal Bhar Bhi Hum Juda Ho, Aisi Saza Na Dena

Tumse Bichadkar, Jeena Na Aayega Humein...
Hum Mar Jaayenge, Kabhi Daga Na Dena...

Muntazir Hai Meri Aankhein, Tere Deedar Ko...
Raat Bhar Jaga Kar, Inhe Thaka Na Dena...

Jidhar Bhi Dekhoon, Bas Tumko Hi Paaon Main...
Nazar Aa Jaaye Mera Aks, Woh Aaina Na Dena...

Raah-E-Ulfat Mein Chal Padhe Hai Mere Qadam...
Ya Rab Manzil Se Pahele Mujhko Qaza Na Dena........

(2)

Tujhe paane k liye mein kuch bhi kar jayunga,
Tere kushi k liye duniya se lad jaunga,
Jis raaste ki tu manzil no ho us raste ko mood jayunga,
Jo faisla na ho tere haq mein usse aaj mein tod jayunga,
Tujhe paane k liye mein kuch bhi kar jayunga,
Teri aankon mein agar dikhe kabhi aansu to,
Un aansun ko aankhon mein aapni bhar k door tujse mein kar jayunga,
Teri raah mein aaye agar kaante to,
Unhe aapne daaman mein samet kar teri raah foolon se bhar jayunga,
Tujhe paane k liye mein kuch bhi kar jayunga,
Tujhe pasand na aaya gar mera yah payar to,
Ek khwaab ki tarah teri zindagi se mein chala jaunga,
Tujhe yaad aaye ya na aaye meri sanam,
Par yeh bhi mumkin nahin k mein tujhe bhul jayunga,
Tujhe paane k liye mein kuch bhi kar jayunga,
Zarurat padi payar mein agar qurbaani ki to,
Yeh shart bhi tujse pehle mein poori kar jayunga,
Is qadar chahat hai teri ki agar tu maang le mujse jaan bhi,
To haste haste yeh jaan bhi mere sanam tere naam kar jayunga,
Tujhe paane k liye mein kuch bhi kar jayunga.

Jyotsna Vyas

Post Graduated In History..
Civil Services Aspirant..
Place Of Residence-Phalodi{Dist.Jodhpur, Rajasthan}
जिंदगी के अनछुए पलों से रूबरू कराने वाली एक गुमनाम शायर
Insta_Id- J_V_Quotes
Yourquotes Id- Jyotsnavyas008

ढलती शाम

ये ढलती शाम...
हाथों से लिखा तुम्हारा वो खत...
मानो मोहब्बत का पैगाम...
साथ में हमसफर चाय का वो जाम...
दुनिया को चाहे अजीब लगे मगर...
हमारे लिए सुकून भरी हसीन शाम....।

तस्वीर

एक तस्वीर-सी बनी है...
दिलों-दिमाग पर तुम्हारी इस कदर...
कि उन्हें शायद चंद शब्दों में बयाँ कर पाना सम्भव नहीं....
चाहती तो कब का भूला देती तुम्हें मगर...
तुम्हारी तस्वीर दिल की दीवारों से मिटती ही नहीं...
अब दिल को भी क्या समझाये साहिब...
सच्ची मोहब्बत की इस झलक को....
यूँ चंद पलों में मिटा पाना भी तो मुमकिन नहीं....

Ankita Arsiya

We try to hide our feelings
but we forget that our eyes speak
I write what I feel

अजनबी'

आंखे बंद हो तो तु नजर आता है
पलकों के खुलते है कहीं खो सा जाता है
नज़रों में बस कर खो जाना
ये एहसास भी कितना प्यारा होता है
अजनबी बनकर कोई इतना खास बने
किसी खूबसूरत सपने का एहसास होता है
Title (writeup 2)
अनदेखा ख्वाब हो तुम,
अनछुआ एहसास हो तुम,
दिल की गहराई मे उतरे हो
इतने खास हो तुम,
हम मिले या ना मिले,
बस पहली नजर का
खूबसूरत नजारा हो तुम,
मेरी जिंदगी का खूबसूरत किस्सा
सच्चाई हो तुम,
अनदेखा, अनछुआ सा ख्वाब
हो तुम.....

Payal Indani

Co- author Payal Indani is a heartborn girl with lots of love in her eyes.. Heartbroken by her loved one.. Still finds love in everyone.. She is happy with whatever she have and also desires to be a author of her own book very soon.. Love legal practices but firmly interested in reality of everything..

Our Love..

The craziest start of our love.. The desperate ones.. You always wanted to be my side. And I always ran away from you.. Rather from your goggles.. You and your goggles were exact opposite.. You with a soft and sweet heart.. And your goggles were scary as ghost.. But the actual thing which made me fall for you.. Were your eyes.. Heartbroken and beautifully beating for me to be with you forever..

Our Love..

We completed a year together.. But still I feel as if I know you from yours.. You have me the thing which no one ever felt of giving.. People either fall in love or they fail in love.. But when it comes to us.. We neither fall.. Nor fail.. We just love.. Unconditionally.. Tru ly.. Deeply and madly for each other.. You are that spark in the darkness which gave me a hope to live again.. You are a miracle and true blessing in my life..

Pooja J. Indani

Co-author Pooja J. Indani is a girl who preserves her relations like gems, she is an hard core painter, a makeup lover, evergreen foodie and writer by hobby. She aspires to complete her doctorate and add prefix Dr. To her name.

Special One

She Was Walking All Alone On Her Path And Then Life Happened And She Came Across A Guy Whom She Never Expected To Meet..
He Made Her Feel Special By His Never Ending Pampering, Chocolates And Old Hindi Romantic Songs. His Voice Made The Magic Spell And Sh e Fell For The Guy To Whom She Never Even Thought Of Talking..
But That's Life..
Yesterday's Stranger Today Became Special One..

Special One

He was silent.., she was talkative..
She was short tempered.., He was calm..
He was shy and she was bubbly..
In every phase they were opposites and yet they never failed to compliment each other..
They stood by each other through every thick and thin and made it worth living..
In true matter they Proved that they are the SPECIAL ONES for eachother...
They shared meaningful silence comfortably..
It is said that Everything Cannot be Verbalize and They were the perfect example of it..

Riya Srivastava

Poet by passion and entrepreneur by action.my word express my feelings and conncet to thefeelings of others.follow me on Instagram@riyashrivastava2000.

खास अजनबी

ज़िन्दगी में उसकी कोई जगह थी नही
पर अचानक से उसकी मौजूदगी का एहसास हुआ
अजनबी ही था वो मेरे लिए
जिससे मुझे बेइंतेहा प्यार हुआ।
न जाना ना ही कुछ समझा
बस उसके आने से एक अलग एहसास हुआ
जिसे जानती ही नही थी कभी
वही मेरे लिए सबसे खास हुआ।
आज ज़िन्दगी बन चुका है वो मेरी
मुझे कुछ इस तरह इश्क़-ए बुखार हुआ
उसकी मौजूदगी से ही
मेरी ज़िंदगी मे खुशियो का आगाज़ हुआ।

Nr. Mrunal Hatwar

She is a student nurse.
Her name is Nr. Mrunal Ramprasad Hatwar
Her instagram ID is @brillarious

(1)

जब तू पास था,
एक अलग सा एहेसास था।
मै अनजान थी,
पर तू तो जनता था।

ज़रा बोलते - बताते,
मुझे भी अपने एहेसासों से महरूम कराते।
तो आज हालात कुछ अलग होते,
शायद हम भी आज साथ होते।

अब तो लगता है,
शायद मै ही गलत थी।
और तू हर पल सही....पर जाने दो,
तब था बचपना और अब है विचारो में गहराई।

पर एक बात कहूं,
किसिके कहोगे तो नहीं।
जब भी तुम्हे देखती हूं,
फील होता है कुछ तो भी।।२×।।

Ritika Nagar

She's Ritika Nagar, a 16 year old girl studying in 11th standard. She loves writing poetries and also have a channel on YouTube for poetries named "Voice of heart". She is from Greater Noida. She participates in many poetry competitions. She has written this poetry on her own and have many more poetries written by her, published on her YouTube channel.

Long Distance Wala Pyaar

Pyaar toh unse hum aaj bhi karte hai,
Unki unn kaatil adao pe ab bhi marte hai,
Dukh nhi agar woh humse dur hai,
Kyuki woh toh hmare dil mein raj karte hai.

Har pal mann rehta unse milne ko bekarar hai,
Mujhe yakeen hai ek din ye dooriyaan,
Nazdeekiyon mein badal jaengi,
Bas uss din ka besabri se intezarr hai.

Wahi meri subah,wahi meri shaam hai,
Har waqt mere labon par rehta usi ka naam hai,
Unke saath zindagi bitana yahi mera khwaab hai,
Kyuki hum toh do jism aur ek jaan hai
.

Biswadeep Sen

A national champion in the field of Karate
A artist who likes to sketch poems with his emotions
A writer who likes to nourish the papers with the ink of his pen and proud member of the Anthology.

My Universe

The Universe tried to hide me from your view,
So, I hid my Universe in you.
Love, your touch is like the blessings of the morning dew,
Painting my life with your warm hue.

Love,just being with you, makes me forget a life so tragic,
For every moment spent with you is no less than magic.
For you were meant to defy logic,
And make me feel ecstatic.

For if castles were made of bones,
You'd be my ribcage and my heart, your throne.
For you were meant to be the light in the dark,
Ever since, becoming my Eternal Monarch.

In my favourite Quadrant of your body
My desire bends in a curve
With two arms
One parallel to your neck
One on your shoulder

Along this slippery curve,
My scuttled scruples
Slide so easily

Some may call it Hyperbola
Some may call it Hyperbole

Prasenjit Raut

Prasenjit raut is an academician. He is currently working as an assistant professor.His life revolves around his family . Being an introvert he found poetry as a medium to express his feeling and tries to bring out the beauty of love.

(1)

चाहे चाँदनी रात हो,
या जेठ की तपती घूप हो,
हर मौसम सुहाना लगे,
जब तू मेरे साथ हो ।

तू मुस्कराए तो सुबह हो,
तेरी उदासी से शाम हो,
मेरी ज़िन्दगी का हर दिन,
बस तेरे ही नाम हो ।

मेरे शब्दों में तू हो,
मेरे एहसासों में तू हो,
मेरे दिल पे, घड़कनो पे,
बस तेरा ही राज हो ।

मेरी हर दुआ में तू हो,
मेरी खुशी और गम में तू हो,
मैं जितनी बार भी ईश्क करूं,
मेरी हर मोह्बबत में सिर्फ तू हो ।।

आशीष "कृष्णा"

बीकानेर जिले के कृष्ण प्रेमी एक शायर और गजल कार जिनका जन्म 2 अप्रैल 2002 को हुआ इनका मूल नाम आशीष कृष्णा है इनका लालन-पालन इनके (फूफा जी) नंदकिशोर जी द्वारा हुआ इन्होंने अपनी उच्च स्तरीय शिक्षा जय भवानी शिक्षण संस्थान से उत्तरण की। इन्होंने अपनी रचनाओं में जिंदगी के अहम हिस्सो को महत्व दिया है ।

"जाम"

अपनी नज़रो से तुमने कमाल कर दिया
मेरे हुजरे में आकर मुझे गुलाम कर दिया।।
मेरी जिंदगी में कहा प्रेम के पन्ने थे
तुमने मेरे हुजरे को प्यार का भंडार बना दिया।।
तेरे महल में मेहमान बन कर आया था
तुमने उस पानी के गिलास को जाम कर दिया।।
ओर जाम के नसे में तुम्हारा नाम तो नही पूछा
मगर तुमने अपने नाम पर मुझे बदनाम कर दिया।

"आँख के आँशु"

आंख के आँशु
जब दिल की
जमीर से उठते है
सारी उदासी व उलझन
ख़ामोशी बनकर
निकलती है
सोचता हूं
इन्हें बिखेर दु
सब जगह
मगर ये भी
नीचे जाकर होठो से
लिपट जाती है
काश !
काश ! इन आँशु की
बूंदों को
बिखेर पाता
ओर बता पाता
दुनिया को
अपना हाल?

Santosh Chawan

My word is my sword.

उसकी कुछ तारीफ़े

तुम ख्वाब नहीं हक़ीक़त हो
वो हकीकत जो एक ख्वाब है
बेवजह मुस्कुराने की वजह हो तुम

आसमान के चाँद तारों सी लगती हो...
मुझे तुम मेरे सपनो में की अप्सरा सी लगती हो...
चाय के ऊपर की मलाई से भी ज्यादा मीठी हो...
तुम्हे चुमू तो मधुमेह सी लगती हो...
तुम खुदा की किसी हूर की परी सी लगती हो..कैसे बताऊं तुझे कि
मुझे तुम कितनी खूबसूरत लगती हो...
मोहबत की है हमने आपसे..
क्यू की आप हमें बेस्ट वूमेन इन द वर्ल्ड लगती हो...
कुछ तो बात है आपके किरदार में ....
पता नही क्यू पर हमें आप लेडी बाहुबली लगती हो..
क्यू तुमे कैद करू इन पन्नो में..
तुम मुक्त ही ज्यादा अच्छी दिखती हो...
तुम्हारी क्या तारीफ़ करूँ..
तुम तो मेरे दिल में नहीं..
मेरी रूह में बसती हो...
मेरी रूह में बसती हो...
मेरी रूह में बसती हो...

Raminder Kaur Mac

Raminder Kaur Mac is Dean – International Affairs at Choithram School, Indore, India where she has been working for the last 23 years. She teaches English to grade 11 and 12 students and looks after the global citizenship programme of the school. In her school she is the Lead Teacher of the business enterprise, facilitator of the TEDEd Club and Curator of the TEDx event. She has received CBSE Teacher Award, Inspirational Teacher Award from School Enterprise Challenge, UK and many other global and national awards. Her creative bent of mind enabled her to be the Editor -in-Chief of the school magazine for eight years. She has a penchant for writing poems and has penned several poems and School Song.

Parents – Our Best Friends

Waking us up
Dressing us up
Providing breakfast hot
Dropping at the bus stop
Juggling with office and work
Responsibilities never to shirk
Helping us complete
All assignments and projects
Preparing for the scary tests
Taking us out on weekends
Fulfilling all our demands
Gifting us the latest cell phone
You are the best friends we've known
Mama I love you, papa I love you!

Growing older
Becoming bolder
Stop communicating
No sharing, start hiding
Indulging in verbal fights
Giving you sleepless nights
Hating your bossism
Your conservatism
Mama I hate you, papa I hate you!

As realization dawns
We let bygones be bygones
Whatever you said
Whatever you pled
Was for our benefit
Teaching us 'never to quit'
Relieving us of the stress
Not to see us depress
Always supporting us
Without a fuss
Wiping our tears

Removing our fears
You are the best friends we've known
Mama I love you, Papa I love you!

Payal Singhal

Payal Singhal is a commerce graduate, a bibliophile, who believes that there is magic in writing, which gives her the liberty to express herself, and most importantly, given the privilege to become soliloquy. She writes to bring a positive impact on societ y, and she knew pen and paper never judge but give a solution and peace every time.

एक लड़का

(मुझे नहीं पता में उसे जानती हूँ या नही)

एक ख़ूबसूरत ख़्वाब की तरह लगता है,
दूर है इसलिए लगता है कि एक सपना है।
बातें करूँ तो वह गाने सुनाता है,
मिलने के मुझसे वह बहाने बनाता है।
नहीं कहता तोड़ ला देगा चाँद वो मुझे,
पर चाँद को देखकर मुझे वो चाँद बताता है
"सफ़र ख़ूबसूरत है मंज़िल से भी" ,
हंसकर मुझे वह बार बार यही समझाता है।
अब तलक भी क़रीब से ना जान सकें हम उसे,
पर फ़ासलों के बावजूद वह क़रीब होने का हर पल एहसास दिलाता है।
शैतान है कभी तो कभी मासूम सा बच्चा सा लगता है,
जैसा भी है वो, न जाने क्यों मुझे बहुत अच्छा सा लगता है?
भूरी आँखें, मुस्कुराहट पे तो कोई दिल वार बैठे
जीत जाएँ हम बस उसको यही दुआ है चाहे फिर ख़ुदको हार बैठे।

Saloni Kumari

Myself Saloni Kumari
Hobby-Reading And Writing (Poetry, Stories), Playing Sports And Games Like Badminton, Chess Etc
Qualification - B. Sc (MATHEMATICS)
I'M AN OPTIMISTIC GIRL
Insta Id- @salonijaiswal78

मन को सम्भालूँ कैसे

मन को सम्भालूँ कैसे
तेरी ओर मुड़ जाता है..
तू दूर है परन्तु...
तेरी सुहावनी यादें..
दिल में नहीं समा पाता हैं|
वो बोलती हुई आँखें..
वो मुस्कुराता चेहरा..
जैसे सुबह में सुरज..
रंग बिखेरता हुआँ..
आसमान में छा जाता है|
वो खड़खड़ाते पत्ते..
मन में हिलोर लाता है..
तेरे आने की जैसे..
मुझको आहट दे जाता हैं|
मन को सम्भालूँ कैसे
तेरी ओर मुड़ जाता हैं....

Ishrat saboon

Ishrat saboon ,she is from Kashmir ,she is a published co - author.she is a student ,a passionate writer and a student with classical dreams and vivid wings.she loves to pen her feelings .she believes that,"A wise man needs some words again as life came out to be vibrating".Her Instagram handle is :Ishratsaboon11 and email id is: ishratsboon@gmail.com

(1)

"Melody of The Meet"
There was something enticing
like the morning breeze
Picturing the growth in falled leaves
For , I learnt the peace
all, where i once
felt the pain

"Kernel Heart"

Winter screaming over the walls ,
OH !shady heart you already hold
fiery glaciers in my head ,
flaming the scented candles
augh ! those memories in the bundle
Screaming...
You are more than enough.
Ishrat saboon

Ganesh Sadashiv Patil

This Is Ganesh Sadashiv Patil From Jalgaon,Maharashtra.He Is The Student Of UG In Field Of Pharmacy.HeIs Writer And Poet Who Writes 150+ Poetry In Hindi And Marathi Languages.He Has Worked In 80 Anthologies As A Coauthour.His Writing Is Also Featured In Pratibha E Magazine.He Is Also Been Part OfVarious Poetry And Writing Competitions At National Level.He Is Part Of World Records Anthologie s.He Is Compiler Of One Anthology Emotions Of Life.He Loves To Write On Love,Humanity, Motivation And SocialThemes. He loves to write down his feelings, his thoughts on various topics which makes him a writer of one his own kind.

प्यार का मिलन

आज का ये दिन निकला बडा हि प्यारा सा है
मन को ये मेरे हर्षित जो यहा कर रहा है
ना जाने कैसी खुशी मेरे जीवन में छा चुकी है
अब काबू ना खुद पर थोडा भी हो रहा है

हम दोनो के प्रेम मिलन का वो दिखेगा नजारा सारा
प्यार की बात करने का वो पल जो आया है
खुलके आज सबके सामने इस प्रेम का मिलन होगा हमारा
किसीसे छुपकर ना मिलने का वो दौर ना आना है

बाते हमारी इतने दिनो की सारी मिलके आज बोहोत होगी
उसपर किसिकी बात ना करणे की कोई पाबंदी होनी है
ना जाने इस दिनके यादमें कितनी थी राते मैने जागी
तब जाकर इतने दिनोके बाद आज वो घडी आयी है

राह में चलते हुए रोज देखता था चुपकेसे जिसे में
चलते हुए उसी जगहपर आज खुद वो राहमें साथ होगी
सच हुई वो ख्वाईश जीससे मिलनके मैने सपने देखे थे
साथ रहेंगे हम दोनो आज वो खुद सामने बैठी होगी

आज वो दिन निकल आया है जीसका हमे इंतजार था
सपने होते सच देखे हुए आज समयका साक्ष होना है

Shivani Shrikant Sarwade

Shivani, an ambitious girl hailing from city of God Vitthal, Pandharpur, Maharashtra who follows her heart and loves to write what her heart says! She is somewhat moody poetess. She has dedicated her career in Pharmaceutical field.
She can sense God in her parents along with that believes in love, kindness and humanity too.
Poetry and art of sketching is her passion, being inspired and motivated by so many well-wishers.

" तुमसे मिलना "

तुमसे मिलना...
मुझे सब कुछ अदा कर जाता है।
तुमसे मिलना...
मुझे मुझसे हि मिलवाता है।
तुमसे मिलना...
मेरे सारे गम भुला देता है।
तुमसे मिलना...
मेरे रास्ते में आनेवाले हर मुश्किल का सामना करने का बल दे जाता है।
तुमसे मिलना...
मरते हुए को भी फिर से जिंदा कर जाता है।
तुमसे मिलना...
प्यार की एक रस्म पूरी होने का एहसास दिलाता है।
तुमसे मिलना...
इस दिल को भी सब कुछ बयान कर देता है।
तुमसे मिलना...
तुमसे मिलने के लिए किया गया इंतजार भी सिखा जाता है।
तुमसे मिलना...
अगली बार आओगे तुम, यही राह देखना सिखा जाता है।

Prakhar Mishra

Prakhar Mishra is an aspiring writer who writes in Hindi, English and Urdu. He has been a part of various anthologies and loves to pour his heart out by poems.
Insta Id-@prakharmishra1403

(1)

Have you ever seen a rose,
That gets more beautiful,
As it grows.

Are you aware of a smile,
So lovely, so cute
And robs your heart with style.

Rightly have they said, that
Love is beautiful, for they
Must have said about you.

All sweet words can be used,
For your lovely black eyes,
That leave me amused.

Your smiling face,
With the cheeks red,
Are most spectacular,
And make me feel blessed.
After all,
You are my love,
Yes ! You are...

Prachi Sharma

She is Prachi Sharma. She lived in Ghaziabad district in U. P. She pursing Bsc maths from CCS UNIVERSITY.
She participated in more than 30 anthologies. She wrote a book FEELING IN WORDS available on Google Play store. She compile three anthologies WRITE TO FEEL NOT TO EXPLAIN , WRITER'S WORLD and FIRST DAY . She participated in Record anthologies and as a co author. She is the founder of KAVYANJALI. This is an online platform who provide opportunities for writers and develop their skills. Give your feedback on email (prachisharma51689@gmail.com). Instagram id (@sharma0162)

Very Special

I am not special for anyone,
But me is very special to myself.
I am not important for anyone,
But very important to myself.
I am not precious for anyone
But very precious to myself.
everyone is to busy
But i am busy for myself.
Everyone trying to happy
But i am trying to happy for myself.
Everyone is trying to put many effort
But i am trying to effort for myself.
Yes I am very special for me.

Akshat Kumar

Akshat Kumar is a student and writer. His writings are related to life musings and inspirations. He is an extrovert, innovative and creative. He always innovates new ideas for his writings.

Love

Love is that chocolate,
Which dissolves you in it, rather dissolving in you.
It makes you feel delighted and make your heart pacify.

' किसी का इंतज़ार '

किसी का इंतज़ार था,
दिल बेकरार था।
माने ना हम वो अजनबी,
दिल उसका साफ़ था।

Mausam Agrawal

She is young writer from Nepal.She has completed her graduation from Kolkata. She writes poems,shayris and stories.

Someone Special

Till the day I met you
I never thought
I will love someone
To the core
You made a place in my heart
Which was special and pure..

You were unique and one of a kind
A pure soul with goodness inside
I found peace in you
Was never afraid to share even the
darkest secrets.

Today when I look back
To the years we were together
I reliase how diffcult it would be
If you were not by my side..

The day I met you
I never thought
You will soon be my someone special.

Aditi Malviya

She is a fun loving and a dreamy person.
She is someone who loves spending time by dancing as a hobby or else reading and also writing these Days.

(1)

Why I love him
He never Stopped blushing when he was Around me,
He was ready to wait for a year,
But never stepped back.

No matter how sad he was, He never failed to put a smile on my face,
I became his priority more than food & water,
I tried pushing him away during my mood swings,
But he returned to pamper me as a kid.

It isn’t easy for him to handle me and his family,
But he manages to balance both,
I know he can fight for me with world
And that is why i love him
And have eyes on only for him.

Muskan Sahu

She is Muskan sahu, a name with smiles and colourful dreams. Obsessed for her writeupps. She is currently a student.Her hometown is raipur chhattisgarh. She is an optimistic late night paper scribbler. Her thoughts are justified to thepeople around . She is passionate for dancing traveling and photography too. Ig handle - @_mushi_._writeupps_

"Dostana Hamara "

Dosti hamari kisi se kam thodi na hai ,
Sabse upar aur mohabbat se badi hai ..
Jab koi ni tha mere pass toh lgta tha koi
toh hota mere pass,
Magar jabse tum aaye ho zindagi me matlab ,
"Everything is so complete"na ,
Aur bharosa ab khudse zyda tum par hai ,
Chahe phir kapde pasand krne ho ya life ke decisions sab kch
start to end tumse hi hota hai ...
Uss rote hue insan ko hasna seekhya ,
Ruthe ko manaya hai , khulkar jeena seekhaya, galat par sahi
bataya aur sahi karne par jo pyar jataya hai na, wo har koi nahi
karta hai..
Isly toh hamari yaari hai sab pe bhari ...
Na koi mashab ki chinta na kisi ke jaane ka gum ,
Hum toh ekdam bindass hai jaise badalo me udhte parinde
ghum...
Abb kya hai na ki , mere paas alfaazo ki kaami hai hamari dosti
baya karne ke liye kyuki hmari yaari ek ehsaas hai jo kisi ki
mohataaj nahi ....
Chidhane ho ya mazak banana dono ko bakhubi aata hai ...
Chahe wo raat ke 3 ya subh ke 3 call hamesha time se uth jata
hai ...
Yaar hume kuch sochne ki jarurat nahi padti jab baat ek dusre
ki aati hai ...
Fir sath me masti karna ho ya ek dusro ko karani ho padhai
sote hue ko utha ke karate hai padhai
khyl krne se lekr pyar krne tak ,
mohabbbat se bhi zyda badhkar ho yaar tum...
mohbbat toh bhula bhi de magar tum,

soch kar bhi darr lagta hai, agar tum nahi hoge toh m apni bakwaas sunaungi kisko, haqq jataungi kispe , ladungi kisse , masti kiske sath karungi aur hasaungi kisko
toh chahe kuch bhi ho jaaye ye dosti hamari sabse alag hai aur hmari wo best tagline #boss_don wo kisi aur ki thodi na ho sakti hai isly toh do anjaan ko upar wale ne jigari jaan banaya hai ..
daulat ki kaami nahi hai mere pass, aakhir tum jo ho mere pass...
Aakhir meri daulat shoharat aan ban shaan toh tum hi ho mere dost ..
aur dosti na hamari sabse badhkar hai,
the only best wali !
toh yaar kabhi bhi kuch bhi ho jaaye do thappad lagakar samjha lenge gale laga kar mana lenge magar ek dusre se kabhi dur nahi jaayenge !!
Aur aakhir ikkrar toh sirf tum se kiya hai mere gdhe ..
Sari cheezo ke liy sukhriya waise sukhriya toh hmari dosti m hota nahi magar fir bhi thankyou for being my backbone at every point of my life love you !

Isha

Isha
A warrior with a warm heart who is ready to fight every situation fearlessly. She is a poet, a writer, a lyricist, and a Shayar, all-in-one. She has been writing since she was a kid. It is as if writing is in her blood and creativity flows in her veins. A girl with a passion for writing, and a curious soul who wants to fly in an open sky using her words. She is a working professional who holds a M aster's Degree in English. She feels that love is the best feeling one can ever experience in life. Her family and friends are her strength. She marks her presence on Instagram as @virtuous_soul17 & @pristinetales.
We hope you will enjoy her creative work. Happy Reading!

This Magical Moment

This moment feels like magic, when,
I take time to pause and observe,
the glory of this beautiful green place!
The immense fascination that is
felt towards the soothing chirping birds
is evident in the eyes of all the beholders!
The timelessness in this streaming river
feeds our human soul to the deepest level.

To turn on its magic,
nature doesn't have to be rare, as
this accord is nested in its magnificent elements!
In the world busy with technology in all its phases,
human beings have lost their connection
with nature & its beauty!

If we spend our time away from technology,
in the arms of nature, we can feel the excitement,
the adventure that it brings to our soul!
To observe nature is an inherent human skill,
which, when developed, can enhance our way
of seeing things in life with positivity & selflessness!

Caterpillars evolving into the beautiful butterflies,
resemble the struggles in our lives,
but their alluring growth justifies the law of nature!
The butterflies embracing the wind with open wings
mirror the freedom that nature provides us
from all the shackles of life and the world!

The fragrance of those roses in a garden
appeases the soul from within!

Those jumping squirrels set our souls carefree
and release all the stress leaving us
smiling to the divine nature & its elements!
The peace that I get while just laying on the grass,
staring at the illimitable sky and those open wings
leaves my soul allayed from all the trammels!

Sweety Akankshya Panda

Sweety Akankshya panda, presently pursuing her graduation in English honours. She is hailing from Bhadrak, Orissa. After the completion of 12th board at Science she started writing quotes, poems and short stories. She believes in reality but for sometimes she lost in her wonder -world.
Insta handle - @feather.of.dreams_

झूठा सपना

कल तक जिससे अपने पास रखी थी,
आज वह बहुत दूर है मुझसे
परेशान सी हूं मैं
आज फिरसे मायूस है मेरी जिंदगी मुझसे,
सोचा नहीं था कि वह भी कभी अपना सा लगेगा,
उसको अपनी वास्तवता के जिंदगी में महसूस करते करते,
पर बिछड़ गया वह क्यों मुझसे!
भगवान ना करे कोई तकलीफ
पहुंचे उससे मेरी वजह से
दुआ करती हूं रब दूर करें सारे तकलीफ उनसे
वे यादें ही काफी है मेरी जिंदगी संवारने की, जिनको मैने संभाल
कर रखी थी एक छोटी सी बैग में जो दिल कहलाता था।

Lost And Found

Innocence flooded all over,
A laugh for an in animate object
a diverse love for her Barbie doll
now lost is taking a toll.

Reminiscing towards the memories spanded,
Sometimes with combing the hair
Sometimes with just loan some talks with it
Rejoicing with once lost true love...

Broken and lost to embers,
A sweet girl of 6 now in distress,
Subtitutes causing no loss in her stress
A never ending cycle of duress....

Akriti Sharma

“ I am Good enough, Smart Enough, Beautiful Enough, Strong Enough. I Believe in these all and so let insecurity run from my life”.

AKRITI SHARMA is a third year student of M.A.Integrated History honours with specialization in cultural and Heritage from School of Social Sciences, Cluster university Jammu. She is from Sunderbani ;District Rajouri ,Jammu. She is interested in writing , painting,singing and dancing. . She love to know more about our culture and researching our heritage sites .She is Orator and Dendrophile person.

Who Is She ?

WHO is she? WHO is She?
The lady who is always with me.
She tells me to speak truth ,
she gave me eyes to see .

WHO is she ? WHO is she?
the lady who is always with me
She is my god ,
She is my inspiration ,
She makes pray for me.

WHO is she? WHO is she?
The lady who is always with me
She fulfill my dreams always,
Her heart is big like Sea.

WHO is she? WHO is she ?
The lady who is always with me
She helped me to learn and think,
She is my knowledge tree.

WHO is she? WHO is she?
The lady who is always with me
She sacrifice her happiness,
And gives happiness to me .

WHO is she? WHO is she ?
The lady who is always with me
She is my success Stair,
She give me world best care
What can I say now further,
The lady WHO is always with me is ‘My Mother’.

Shivani Priyanga

Shivani Priyanga, a young writer, an engineer from the foot of our mom India "Tamil Nadu".
She loves scribbling love!
She loves sketching pure!
She loves sculpturing story!
Just with her words!!
She had worked as Co-author in number of anthologies.
And there is a secret about her,
She is in love with words
Mail: shivanipriyanga@gmail.com
Instagram: shivani_priyanga_quotes
Yourquote: Shivani Priyanga

The Rain Writes

At the time,where the sun smirks,
In between the dark clouds...
Dusky sand spreads Fragrance!
I am standing in the balcony,
Seeing the birds kidding me!
Found the remembrance of of of.....
Am totally off!
Tasted the cup of coffee and also you in the next sip!
Heart starts the dance!
Skin scatters the Goosebumps!
Eye portraits behind scene clipages!
Unknowingly, ears hear you!
And I am completely hypnotised!
Spontaneously and simultaneously everything happens....
In the mixture of faintest heart and confused brain,
I want to feel it even more!
Sitting on the chair,
Having you in my thought!
The best ever poem it is!
A change is felt in the upper-space,
The clouds are I eager to know our secret...
It is sending spy;
Raindrops climbed over me!
The chilness ask,
"Who you are thinking of?"
Red cheeks reply,
"It is him"
The rain , the cloud and the birds conflicts a confusion!
The coffee cup shatters!
Tongue dramatically dances our story!
All are mesmerised,
In the sand,

With the huge ink,
Clouds sculptured our story as a Novel!
It completes our love story in an hour...
I am in the mode of crore blushes!
Now,
The cloud vanishes,
The same birds complement us!
Then,
The last page of the novel is completed with a Rainbow which started in my lips...
I had a higher view on the search of that cloud...
With a huge thunder,
"I'll come again to see you both again"
Thus the rain writes once again!!!

Priyanka Sharma

I am a student of BA.
I am a struggling writing and acting.
I love to do Audio poetries and video editing.
My aim is to be a writer and actress.

अहसास जज्बातों ने किया

1. कभी फुर्सत मिले तो साथ बैठना,
तुम्हें अपने दिल का हाल बताएंगे,
हर पल तुम्हें याद करते हैं,
वो एहसास आज हम तुम्हें दिलाएंगे।।।

2. कभी भीड़ में कभी तनहाई में,
कभी आंखो की भीड़ में,
तुझे ढूंढते ढूंढते कहा आ गए है हम,
कहीं घूमने तो नहीं तुझ से रूबरू होने आ गए है हम।।।.

प्यार लफ्ज़ों में कहा

1. दूर रहती हूं◌ँ मगर दिल के करीब हो तुम मेरे,
खास हो इसलिए तुम मेरी शायरी के अल्फ़ाज़ हो,
दरबदर भटकती हूं◌ँ तुम्हें याद करते हुए,
कैसे इज़हार करूं अपनी मोहब्बत का ये बात अपने दिल में दफनाए रखती हूँ।।।।

2. इशारों में समझ जाते हैं कैसे दिल के ये रिश्ते हैं,
अल्फाजों को बांध के किसी पोटली में रख दो,
बस इत्र-ए-गुलाब से मेरे ज़ेहन में बसे रहो,
थाम के हाथ मेरा मुझे अपने ख्वाबों में ले चलो।।।

Gurdeep Kaur

Writer, poetry lover
Insta Id-deep13.gk

Far Love

Moon is far away from Earth
But people Love it
Sun is far away from Earth
But people pray it
Stars is far away from Earth
But people study on it
Sky is far away from Earth
But birds fly in it
Metal are deep in Earth
But people find it
Rain fall from sky
But people bath on ground
Leaves fall from tree branches
But come again too
No matter how far your partner is
But he /she love like u r with them

Love

Love can bring dead to life
Love can make people strong
Love is world's best feeling
Love can also make people cry
Love can make people believe
Love can spoil the people
Love can make people dreams come true
Worst thing of love is it make people blind

Komal Singh

Komal Singh was born on 19 June 2004. Co author is a good writer from New Delhi. She is completing her schooling in commerce stream. She is writingquotes or stories since 1 year as her passion. She wants to be Writer and Bank PO.

"Love Is Something In Which We Should Live Happily Not Forcefully."

Love has infinite definitions. Everyone defines love how or what they feel. According to me, "Love is something which is undefinable." It is a strong affectionate feeling that you have when you like somebody or something so much. Love can be defined in so many languages. Like in German we say liebe in Dutch we can define love as liefd in French as i'amou r etc. Love is an emotion from which we have made our self. There can be so many types of love like: - self - love , Affectionate love , Familiar love , obsessive love , selfless love etc.

Self - love means taking care of your own needs and not sacrificing your well - being to please others. Self - love means caring of yourself. Self - love can be expressed by prioritising yourself, trusting yourself, thinking about yourself rather than others, Being nice and kind to yourself. You can also indulge in me time which means giving time to yourself. You should accept yourself as you are. You should not see yourself in the fear of being judged by your physical appearance, your opinions, work etc. Self - love can motivate you to live a healthy and peaceful life. You will start loving yourself when you take care of you.

Stop comparing yourself to others. I know everyone's opinion matters but when it is about you create your own opportunities as no one will do it for you .

Everyone can express self love but you kn ow what, a mother and a father cannot do self love because they don't think about themselves, they think about their children and their family . Everyone knows mother's love is unconditional . Mother will not eat anything but then also she can provide nutr itious food to their children . A father can sacrifice his needs for their children .

Every relation is god gifted by birth but only the friendship is made by us by choosing right or deserving person in our life. Friends play some role in everyone's life but during teenage friends play a major role. At this age, friends are in love with each other. They share each and every thing of their life. They are attached or engrossed in each other because parents or siblings sometimes don't understand what they ne ed. They don't understand one's feeling so friend is their to understand that from how much they go through. At the teenage people often meet so many loved ones which are sometimes forever and sometimes for months or years .

"Love is done by heart , not by blood ,skin tone , gender or caste."

Reshma Sultana

She is a teacher, writer and social worker. She is passionate about writing.she believes that through writing one can heal its pain. Poetry can change the world ---believing in this thought she includes poems and articles in her pen.She has already given her essence of writing in some books like "Spasms of emotion ",Dil ka sukoon -Meri maa, same one Special, "Cosmetic Element ".She prefers simple words to craft her writing which makes her writing Unique

Longing For Someone

Someone To be true...to me
Whether near or far apart,
whose love will always be there
As a treasure in my heart.

To need a helping hand
Who take care and understand

To make me think,laugh or smile
When I am down,it picks me up
If only for a while......

To have someone... in my life
Listen my silence in a while

You are like refreshing breeze
Making sure... I feel at ease
Someone like you is like rainbow Fair
Who cherish my life with care

Love-The Healing Emotion

I felt love.... When I lost you.
I felt love when ignored by you.
When things went wrong i felt Love for you. To forgive is love and to accept my flaw are love.The magic of love sweeps you up your feet and keep you in a state of ecstasy. Life has been very hard and at the same time it has taught me a great deal .A relationship exist in loyalty and trust.Once broken cannot be retained."The falling",the breaking "and" the healing "is what supposed to happen to us. The sun loves moonso much he died every night to let her breath.This is the depths of love. The love In the mirror may make you stronger but the reflects your heart that can make you true.The love that takes away your sadness and calms you is just as deep as an ocean. Everything is temporary but love outlives us all .So Cherish your life with love .People seem to forget how beautiful it is to grow old with someone,to build and witness someone's progression and conquer obstacles with all together instead of facing them alone.I understand its really impossible now a days to count on someone with all your heart and soul.If then anything I guess that's why you can count me as one of the rare ones.I am not in it for a reason or season.I am in it for life time.

Tanvi Jamwal

Tanvi Jamwal is a third year student of Integrated M.A in History with specialization in Cultural Heritage, Cluster University Jammu. She is from J&K. She is more into doing creative things. She loves doing Photography, writing and Dancing. She is Doing Research on Intangible Heritage. Now she also runs a instagram page to showcase her Photography Skills by the name: A lasting impression (lens.queen16)

मेरे प्यार हो तुम

दूर होकर भी मेरे पास हो तुम
नीरस ज़िंदगी की आस हो तुम।

एक मीठा, सुहाना एहसास हो तुम
मेरी जिंदगी के लिए खास हो तुम।

करूं प्यार जिसे बेशुमार हो तुम
हर पल करूं जिसका दीदार हो तुम।

मेरी इक इक सांस है तुम्हारी
तुम्हारी हर बात मुझे लगती है प्यारी।

मेरी प्रार्थना में तुम, मेरी दुआओं में तुम
मेरे ज़िक्र में तुम,मेरे फिक्र में तुम।

तुझको ना देखूं तो ना आता चैन है
तू ही मेरा दिन तू ही मेरी रैन है।

प्यार से भी प्यारे हो तुम
मेरे जीवन के सहारे हो तुम।

मेरे चांद,सूरज,सितारे हो तुम
मेरे ख्वाबों के सुंदर नज़ारे हो तुम।

होते हो जब पास मेरे तब होती हूं पूरी
तुम बिन मेरी जिंदगी है बस अधूरी।

तुम्हारे साथ ही मेरी हर खुशी जुड़ी है

हर राह मेरी तेरे संग ही तो मुड़ी है।

कल अजनबी थे आज खास हो तुम
मैं खुशनसीब हूं कि मेरे पास हो तुम।
मेरी आदत हो तुम
मेरी ईबादत हो तुम
मेरी जान हो तुम
मेरी मुस्कान हो तुम
अपने से भी ज़्यादा जिसे किया है प्यार वो तुम।
मेरे प्यार हो तुम
मेरे प्यार हो तुम।

Utkarsh Devale

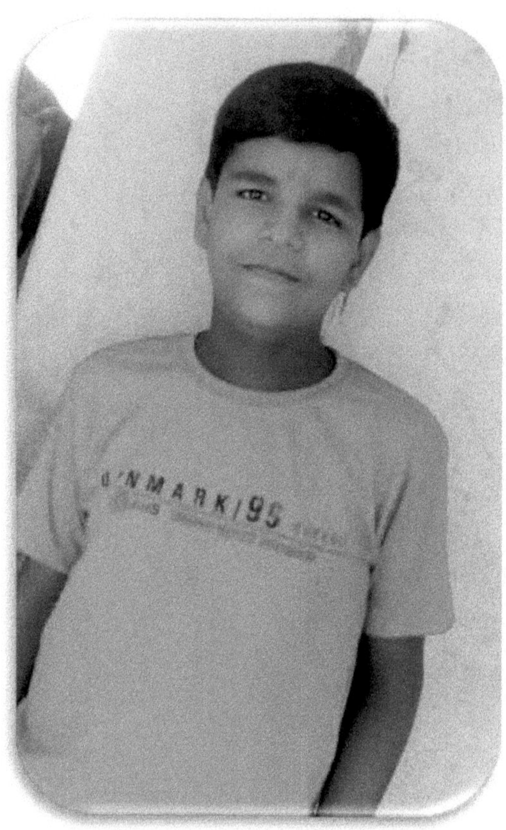

He is a student learning in 8th standard. He found of learning new science experiments along with sketching also. Sometimes he tries to express himself in poe tic words. He is hailing from the holy city, Pandharpur.

वह माता है

वह है अंधेरे मे उजाला ,
वह है हर प्रश्न का उत्तर,
वह है संकट मे आधार,
वह है ताले की चाबी,
वह है दिल का खून,
वह है नकारात्मकता मे सकारात्मकता,
वह है निराशा मे आशा,
वह है खेत मे उगने वाली फसल,
वह है इंसान का जीव,
वह है माता.

Maniska Das

Maniska has some scripted desires in her writing, and has a good way to express it simply. At the young age of 18, she had worked already as co-authors of more 3 Anthologies. She finds it an amazing way for her experience and her passion writing. She belongs to the holy city Puri,Odisha,India seeking the blessings of Shri Jagannath and sharing love.

As Gustave Flaubert said, "The art of writing is the art of discovering what you believe." S o, she hopes you all will discover profoundness of this art.

Reliving Flashbacks

On a rainless weather,
With the dusky winds,
I wonder;
How life turned about?!

It was a new year beginning,
When I drenched a heavy Goodbye!
Which was unable for doing back in days,
Getting free of all burden since years,

I knew it's a new spring;
Still uncertain if the life will blossom,
Didn't thought you're the strength within,
Unknowingly where I drowned in.

A new start, a fresh day;
A new feeling; a new rain,
It wetted me, oops us!
In the very first rain of love.

All these things are so far away,
Like just a magical dreaming,
Yet I've to pinch my receptors,
For getting to know I'm in senses.

You were that blessing,
Which God gifted me without demanding,
Maybe he just compelled you as my someone special,
To overcome my solitariness with peck of warmth.
On a soundless night,
When I lift a pen to write;
I don't know the emotions behind,
But it gave a smug smile insight

Priyanka Yadav

Currently I'm pursuing graduation from Delhi University.
I'm From Orai (Jalaun) Uttar Pradesh.
Writing is my passion.
I believe that Everything is possible in this world.

"मां"

क्या लिखूं तुझ पर "मां"
तू तो ममता की मूरत है,

तुझसे ही मेरी पहचान और तुझ से ही तो मेरा सारा जहान है,

मेरे हर अच्छे बुरे पल में मेरे साथ हमेशा रहता तेरा ही तो प्यार है,

तेरे होने से ही तो मेरी ज़िन्दगी में खुशियों की बहार है,

मेरे हर सपने को हकीकत बनाने में साथ तेरा बेशुमार है,

तेरे होने से ही तो मेरा ज़िंदगी का हर दिन खास है,

तुझ पर और क्या लिखूं "मां"
तू ही तो मेरी ज़िन्दगी का सार है...!!

2)- बड़ी महंगी है ख्वाहिशें हमारी,
ज़िंदगी के हर दौर में हम तुम्हें अपने साथ चाहते हैं...!!

3)- हमारी दीवानगी में कुछ कसूर उनका भी है,
क्या करें वो अगर इतने प्यारे ना होते
तो हम भी इस कदर उनके दीवाने ना होते...!!
"तुम्हारे साथ चलना है"

रास्ते कैसे भी हो "जाना"
मुझे तो तुम्हारे साथ चलना है,

जो देखा था कभी हमने मिलकर
अब हर वो ख़्वाब पूरा करना है,

किए थे जो मोहब्बत में वादे
अब हर उस वादे को सच करना
है,

कोई दुःख छू भी ना सकें तुम्हें
अब हर उस दुआ को मुकम्मल करना है,

तुम्हारी आंख से निकले हर आंसू को
अब मुझे अपनी आंखों का काजल बनाना है,
हालात कैसे भी क्यों ना हो
पर अब तो मुझे अपनी ज़िन्दगी का हर सफ़र तुम्हारे साथ तय करना
है,

हां! जाना मुझे तो तुम्हारे साथ ही चलना है...!!

Agrima Viraj

She has completed her schooling in the year 2020 and is currently preparing for the competitive exam NEET. She is highly determined to pursuit her profession as a DOCTOR. The writer within her awakened when she started penning down her boundless thoughts & emotions. Her poetries generally incline towards the moderation, tenderness and teenage insight of living life. Also she can very portray herself to the readers through her writings and expres s the hidden contemplations within her.

To read her poems more, follow her on
Instagram: @agrima_viraj
YourQuote: Agrima Viraj
You can also read her blogs on:
www.theuntouchedmind.wordpress.com

काश तुम होते

फर्क़ है पास रहने में और साथ होने में
डर है बस उस ख्याल से, तुझे खोने में
आस है तुझसे मिलने कि किसी कोने में
कुछ पल ही सही बस तेरे करीब होने में

वो लोग कहते हैं प्रेमी होते मुसाफिर हैं
साथ ही चलते साथ ही मंज़िल पाते हैं
रब से दुआ है कि काश तुम पास मेरे होते
और काश ना होते ये अनजाने◌ समझौते

मुझे सीने से लगाने के लिए काश तुम होते
मुरझाए चेहरे को हँसाने के लिए पास होते
इंतज़ार ना हुआ कोई अरसा हो गया जैसे
मानो इम्तिहान दरमियान है हमारे कुछ ऐसे

बातें बहुत हैं मगर सुनने के लिए तुम नहीं
माना ज़रिये बहुत हैं कहने सुनने के लिए
दिल बेकाबू हो इससे पहले मिलना कहीं
सब्र किए खड़ी हूँ, होठों पर तेरा नाम लिए

Avneet Kaur

She is a girl who let her writing express all the intense emotion she feel

Dear Self

Hey, how you doing? Are you okay?
I know you don't take care of yourself and pretend that you are just fine
Always trying to help others but when someone offer you help, you just deny
You gotta understand something
Anyone else's problem or discomfort isn't your thing
You are an individual, make sure you are alright
Everyone else can take care of themselves and win their own fight
You don't have to be there for everyone else when you're tearing apart yourself
Nobody gonna give a damn about you, if you lose yourself
You aren't born to take care of others
I know, you are just nice but you can't let people use you as of their needs
How can you help people when you ignore your own troubles
I know, you are strong, baby girl but sometimes it's okay to stop pretending
Chase your own dreams and stop running
You are an amazing being, with or without people's validation
Help yourself, the way you help others, with same dedication

The One

I know I haven't met my right one yet
I am in no hurry either, and I don't even regret
Being in love is an immense feeling, I never got to experience
But I know a person, who feel known yet is mysterious
The one that lives in my head rent free
Somehow that person feel more close than everyone else
Maybe I'm in love with that person, I won't disagree
The feeling I get thinking of that person is great, itself
I don't know ifIf I will ever meet that person or it will just stay in my imagination
It's a possibilty that they just live in other nation
I dont regret keeping them in just my own reality , they feel closer to my heart
I know that's the only who won't hurt
I would tell them that I love them, if I could
So I just wrote it down cause that's the only thing that feels good

Pooja

My name is pooja iam from Delhi
My hobbies is to make portey&art an craft
I want to become a professional writer

Pyaar

Ajj se pehle aisa na hua
Per ajj dil hai ki kuch maang lu
Ye ek patthar nahi uska tukda tujhse ye puch raha hai
Pata nahi kyu par ajj iss soye hue tukde ko jeene ka mann sa hua hai

Ajj tu bas mujhpe barasja
Teri halki bundo ka bhar mujhe bhi sehna hai

Main to bas tutkar tujhme bikharna chahta hu
Main bhi sabki tarah tera mol samjhna chahta hun
Tujhe barste dekh sab bolne lagte hai
Wese main bhi apni chuppi tujhme todna chahta hun

Ab kaise kahu tujhse itna or jo saalo se na keh paya
Ab kaise kahu tujhse itna or jo saao se na keh paya
Ab khud hi samjh ja na ki main tujhme Kitna dubna chahta hun

Himanshu Ranjan

Himanshu Ranjan hails from the heart of Jharkhand,Ranchi.He loves to pen down his thoughts and emotions.He lo ves writing and is currently a student,started writing from the age of 10 while he was in 4th Std
Beside writing he loves music and plays guitar and flute as well. He is a student of life sc ience and has a keen interest in observing and understanding human behaviour anatomy and physiology.

मेरा पहला प्यार

वो पहली मुलाकात
बचपन की वो बात
अस्पताल का वो माहौल
और किलकारी मेरी आवाज़

तेरी प्यारी सी मुस्कान और
आंखों में एक अलग ही चमकान
वो स्नेह से भरा आंचल
ममता का वो एहसास

तेरी हर बात प्यारी सी लगती थी
तेरी हर डांट दवाई सी होती थी
कड़वी थी मगर कुछ नया सिखाती थी
कुछ बतलाती कुछ समझाती
मगर हर पल सत्य ही होती थी

मेरे हर सवालों का जवाब
होता था तेरे पास
मेरे हर इशारों को पकड़ने
की कला होती थी तेरे पास

बस तू ही समझती थी मुझे
प्यार करती थी दुलारती थी
पर जरूरत परने पर फटकारा भी
तुम ही करती थी

हर मुश्किल से थी तुम मुझे बचाती
मेंरे पथ की कठनाइयों को तुम विष समझ
संभू शंकर सा पी जाती
तुम से ही मैंने प्यार को जाना
तुमने ही मुझे उससे पहचान करवाया
आंख खोला तो पहली दफा तुझे ही पाया
तेरे सामने शीश नवाया

मां तुम से मैं आज ये कहता हूं
प्यार मैं सिर्फ तुम्ही ,सिर्फ तुम्ही से
करता हूं
मेरा पहला प्यार हो तुम
मेरा पहला प्यार हो तुम

Ashis Pahi

Ashis Pahi, pursuing Master degree in Commerce (Accounts), and regular writer in YourQuote platform since 2017. He loves to write poems, shayari, quotes, and spare my time in reading novels and try to learn differen t languages of his country. He strongly believe in himself. His determination is much more important than dedication..

My Love For Tiger And Brownie

Love doesn't mean it should be between two persons who can convey and communicate their feelings foreach other. Love is an emotional attachment that can happen with all of us to any human being, an animal. I'm here to narrate my love towards my two pet dogs to whom I call Tiger and Brownie.

My father brought Tiger when he is 2 months old and since he is with us and I treat him like my boy. He even shows his love, gratitude, affection for me. He loves to play with me I feel bad for Tiger that he can't speak but he can hear what I'm saying? When Tiger came to our home after few days Brownie came to our home to play with Tiger. Brownie is the elder brother of Tiger. When they both walk on the road nobody prefers to come in between them. Both are aggressive but Tiger is highly aggressive. Their love for me I have no words to define. They proved their loyalty s ince the existence of human life started in this universe.

Like all humans need love and affection with proper care similarly animals need your love, care, and affection for their life.

Priyanshi Mittal

Priyanshi, An enthusiastic writer who writes to pour her heart to the world to aspire it with her own experiences and feelings. Decorates her words with the depth of her heart and she believes that life is a journey with vivid twists and turns to be explored in every moment.
Ig id: _soul_ful_poetry_

Love - A Beautiful Imagination

The curtains close
In a single sight
My eyes are still on collen in white.
I imagine her dancing
Holding my hand in twilight.
A lot of words were going on in my mind
Despite my lips were quiet.
My breathe hold on and lose consciousness
Ran towards the stage
But the curtains were closed
My story holds there!!
I want to rewrite
This time with all my might.

Navjot Singh

Navjot singh, an aspiring author and a physiotherapist has worked on multiple anthologies including Chimera and Vibgyor also projects including the famous Harry Potter fan fiction, "Harry Potter And The Curse Of The Lying Prophecy." And 165-B Resident .
He loves to write about nature, love and self worth.
Author can be reached on his Instagram
@the_vintage_soul
Email- nj970816@gmail.com

Feeling Close.

We have been together for not so long,
The bond between us may not be strong,
But we try to understand and adjust,
To keep it fresh and prevent from dust,
I remember the moment i held your hand,
I felt like I have enough power to stand,
To stand against the world for you,
Just need these feelings to subdue,
I remember when we held hands for first time,
No words are enough to explain or even to create a rhyme,
I know you were cautious and your heart beat rose,
It was great I really felt we are close....

Your Heart Beat..

It is very less when someone touches one's soul,
That was the moment I found my role,
The role to keep you safe,
From the pain the world always gave,
Holding you in my arms was like heaven,
I didn't even realise that it was past eleven,
The wind was blowing, the love it was showing,
Was at epitome, the streetlights started to deplete,
When I felt a surge in you heartbeat,
It rose and then settled at a normal pace,
May be you saw the confirmation on my face,
That i am here, here for you,
The words aren't enough but yes,
I LOVE YOU

T. Priyadharshini

She's Priyadharshini. Mommy's girl. The person she loves the most in her life is her mom. Pursued her masters in English literature. She was about to kickstart her PhD. She's adie-hard disciple of Bruce Lee. A language lover she's. Certified in Japanese language. Her happiness is giving soul to her contemplations and inking it down. A budding writer and a movie lover too.

Love At First Feel

Love...
It is a magic spell which casts happiness,
It is a stroke of luck in everyone's life,
It cessates one's melancholic weep and,
Makes someone grin like a cheshire cat,
It is a soothing panecea to someone's scar.

Love is like a wind,
It can waft anywhere without any boundaries,
It doesn't cognize about caste and religion,
It is universal and ubiquitous,
Love is winsome but, a 'Mother's love' is priceless.

Mother's love is unique and unconditional,
Mother's love is inspiring and infinite,
Mother's love is sweet and soulful,
Mother's love is pure and pristine,
Mother's love is angelic and altruistic.

She started loving you, even before you touch this world;
She started loving you, even before holding you in her hands;
She started loving you, even before you open your eyes;
She started loving you, even before seeing your face;
She started loving you, the moment she felt you in her womb.

Love at first feel...
Dedicated to my mom.

Vishal K R

Vishal is a poet , avid reader , creative writer and a future doctor who hails from Bangalore. A 20 year old , He had won second prize in poetry competition conducted on World Tuberculosis Day. Being an introvert , he focuses on improving self skills and his vocabulary in English .He also likes to read books and write poetry in his free time. He follows his hobbies with passion and enthusiasm and often questions himself which are thought provoking indeed.

Celebrate Love

O'er the armchair she sat ,
Remembering various marriages on rock ,
How on Earth our relationship's strong ?
Yoke not broken , still fresh from that day,
Yonder she saw , a man in dark , frail and in a green jacket , a book in his hand , her beloved engrossed in it. Oh boy !
Diamond jubilee celebration isn't for all ,
I'm one among the lucky few.
Ages have pa ssed , yet he looks the same , reflection from heart isn't the same like mirror.
What's the secret behind this ? When questioned , pat came the answer.
The 3D's , Derailment , Doubt , Disturbance , leave it in the Dustbin , so our marriage will be as beaut iful as the ones in dock.
Derailing our coach of marriage , Doubt about one's vows he gave at marriage , Disturbing factors that can come in form of conspirators , leave the thoughts in trash and life goes smooth.
She takes the load you carry , let's be equal. Mother's love can never be achieved , Umbilical relation is strong , but the relation you get after exchanging the ring , the mother gives her child to another woman to take up her role , much stronger than before.

What Is Love ?

A emotion so strong that cannot be measured by any means. A mystery no man is able to solve.
Love , built on looks and wealth , will become flimsy for looks can be deceiving and will not stay for long.
But , a love built on mutual trust and understanding stays longer and fresher , no matter how old an individual is.
Doubts , mistrust and ego must be kept at bay as it spoils the sanctity of love. A true love only becomes more strong at a distance , for they understand each other in a better way , change their way of approach and will suit the needs of their spouses. On the other hand , ungrateful people also exist who take advantage of love and make others emotionally fragile. If a person is of a loving nature , garbed in a rough appearance , only a handful of people close to them can understand as they're not a person who showcases love in a usual way like others do. Their love can only be understood if you put yourself in their shoes. They don't show love openly , it takes time for them , but the ones closest to them would realise that they're the best lovers to ever exist. Ancient tales have a gallery of love to tell , from the Greek era of Baucis and Philemon to the modern love of King Edward viii and Wallis Simpson, who gave up his throne for Love !!! Reflection on mirror is erroneous , reflection on heart matters the most !!!
Love can be direct or indirect the message it conveys will always be the same , mother embraces you , father makes sure he gets the best for you , both are love , way of showcasing is different.

Aditi Kumari

She is Aditi kumari .She is doing her B.Sc in biotechnology from Xavier college ,ranchi .She started her first writing in Vth standard . She loves to write poems ,writeup ,quotes and minitales.

(1)

"LOVE " is the word that holds thewhole universe in it . When you love someone ,you see only good sides of them ,when you love them even their flaws ,their mistakes looks adorable . Love makes life like a fantasy dream world . Love makes everything beautiful like a flower . Love makes one brave enough to fight for their loved ones .Life needs love like heart needs a beat .But before loving anyone else ,love yourself first .Love yourself for what you are ,for being beautiful in every shape ,every colour . When you start loving yourself ,thenyou can give love to others more than anyone can . Love yourself as certain dark things are to be loved ,in secret ,between the shadow and soul. When you truely love someone ,you don't need to think twice before being vulnerable in front of them . Love is the most comfortable place you can be by truely being yourself .

"LOVE IS NOT LOVE UNTILL LOVE IS VULNERABLE."

(2)

My heart beat get stopped for a moment ,when I saw him. Standing on the opposite side of the road ,holding umbrella .He was like a dre amcatcher who is holding my all dreams . He was looking like a beautifull angel ,the lightest feather who is flying in air just for me . A beautifull flower bud in the dessert ,giving hopes to others - that monsoon will come soon , that the dry dessert wil l be green one day . my love of life was in front of me standing beside the road .

Love at first sight doesn't need any logic within it ,when the moment when you find your "better half" the whole world is going to rotate 360° completely .

He is the brightest star of the sky , hiding all my darkness in his bright lights . He transformed me into a beautifull butterfly from a caterpillar.

He is my galaxy , my whole world revolves around only him . He is my first love and he will be .I need him like a desse rt needs rain .

Himanshu Chaturvedi

As a poem writer Himanshu Chaturvedi is a person of writing the reality of society with his creative mindfulness and with little texture of humour.He also wrote on different topics of love, Friendship, Maa, Nation and many more and his greatest quality is to write the truth in his writings with humanitarian behaviour. We wish him for his long journey in writing......

!!सिया-राम!!

क्या होता है प्रेम ये न जानते थे हम..
रामायण ने हमें यह समझा दिया...
सीता ने धर्म नहीं छोड़ा...
और राम ने सारे सुखों का परित्याग किया...

रहेंगे सदा ये दोनों प्रेम के परिचायक....
एक ने सूपनखा के प्रस्ताव को ठुकराया....
तो दूसरे ने लंका को त्याग दिया....

क्या होता है प्रेम ये न जानते थे हम..
रामायण ने हमें यह समझा दिया।।

।।सिर्फ तुम।।

समय के रिवाज़ कह गए....
बदलते लिवाज़ कह गए....
जीने के अंदाज़ कह गए...
सिर्फ तुम सिर्फ तुम....

तोडा़ हमें वक्त के पहिये ने...
दुखाया है दिल ऐसे रवैये ने...
तुम हमें खुश-मिजाज़ कह गए....
सिर्फ तुम सिर्फ तुम....

Husaina S

She is Husaina S, from Kanniyakumari,India..Her father is Mr.Shakir Hussain. Husaina is a sincere,hardworking,talented girl, who is just 20 years old doing UG course in English Literature, but She concentrates more on developing her skills, especially her passion "Poetry and Writing " Her works were published in more than five Anthologies..She is also compiling two books! One of her work was published in a famous tamil magazine named "Valari". Two Months back, One of her Poem was recited in the Germany FM. She is the Editor for two Magazines "Veeratamil" and "Vilvam". She is also working as "Head" for Magazines in Nanjil Anand Foundation.

My True Love

Love Love
Oh My Love!!
I'm back to My
Old Memories...
Where I was in
My Mom's Womb!
She haven't seen me..
She haven't touched me
She only feel me...
She also feed me
Through the food
She consumes...
She listened My Heart Beat
Through her Heart Beat!
She lost her sleep
To make me feel safe!
She ate Medicinary
To Safeguard me from Infectionary!
She loves me then
Now and Forever!

Flairs and Glairs, a platform by a student for the students. We are esteemed youth struggling to carve out our path for our future and we follow a basic mindset Since everyone is not born with all-round skills. Joining hands with people who are born to execute it with perfection is the best way to evol ve. Self-Evolution is the need of the hour but, evolving as a community is what we strive for. The initiative as kickstarted by, Founder - Mr. Shubham Shah with the motive to utilize the skillset and talent of writing has now a team of 10+ people who are actively participating into newer forms of learning and discovering talents among youngsters. We Provide platform and services like Publishing opportunities, Open mics, Workshops, Hands-on training. Operating with Brand Name of Flairs and Glairs (Publication House), we offer the chance of elevating a passionate writer to an esteemed author With Brand name Teekhe Zasbaaat. We bring to you an opportunity to get accustomed with the Public Speaking and Presenting of Thoughts along with regular challen ges to brush up your inking spirit. The newest initiative to extend our services we introduced in a new writing Platform- The Glittering Fables and Ink Over Tears.

We Choose to Fly Like A Falcon than to be

a Leg Pulling Crab.

To Know More: Infoline – 7781900870
Mail Us At-
flairsandglairs@gmail.com / info@flairsandglairs.in
Or Visit is at
www.flairsandglairs.com / www.flairsandglairs.in
Social Handles- @flairsandglairs @teekhezasbaaat

www.ingramcontent.com/pod-product-compliance
Ingram Content Group UK Ltd.
Pitfield, Milton Keynes, MK11 3LW, UK
UKHW022005190726
13853UKWH00004B/1741

9 789391 302016